DEMCO

Sleeping Cutie

Andrea Davis Pinkney   ILLUSTRATED BY Brian Pinkney

Gulliver Books • **Harcourt, Inc.**   Orlando Austin New York San Diego Toronto London

To Chloe and Dobbin
—A. D. P. and B. P.

www.HarcourtBooks.com

Gulliver Books is a trademark of Harcourt, Inc., registered in
the United States of America and/or other jurisdictions.

Library of Congress Cataloging-in-Publication Data
Pinkney, Andrea Davis.
Sleeping Cutie/Andrea Davis Pinkney; illustrated by Brian Pinkney.
p. cm.
"Gulliver Books."
Summary: Cutie LaRue is perfect in nearly every way, but her
sleeplessness causes problems for her parents until they send
for a new toy that introduces Cutie to the Dreamland Nightclub.
[1. Sleep—Fiction. 2. Owls—Fiction. 3. Nightclubs—Fiction.] I. Title.
PZ7.P6333Sl 2004
[E]—dc21   2002014376
ISBN 0-15-202544-8

First edition
H G F E D C B A
Printed in Singapore

The illustrations in this book were done in Sumi brush,
pen and ink, and colored inks on watercolor paper.
The display type was set in Mona Lisa.
The text type was set in Mercurius Medium.
Color separations by Bright Arts Ltd., Hong Kong
Printed and bound by Tien Wah Press, Singapore
This book was printed on totally chlorine-free Stora Enso Matte paper.
Production supervision by Sandra Grebenar and Ginger Boyer
Designed by Lydia D'moch

Cutie LaRue was a darling. Adorable. Sweet as cream.

She always cleaned her plate.

She put away her socks.

She brushed her teeth
three times a day.

Yes, Cutie was very agreeable. She hardly complained.
She never fussed. And whining was not her style—except
at bedtime.

That's when Cutie became downright defiant.
She shook her head. She stomped. She hollered loud
enough to rattle the window blinds. "I'm *not* tired!"

Cutie's parents tried everything to make her sleepy.

Warm milk.

Bubble baths.

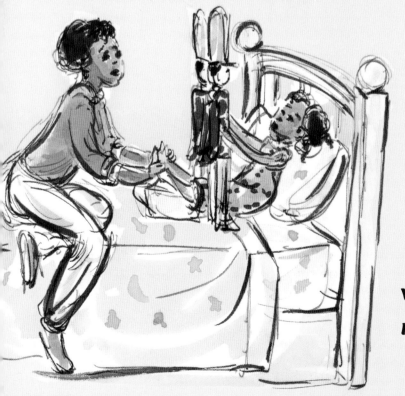

Foot rubs.

Nothing worked. Cutie's cry was the same every night. "I'm *not* tired!"

Truth be told, Cutie *wasn't* tired and she didn't sleep.

She called out for a drink of water. She practiced her jumping jacks. One night she even rearranged her bedroom furniture.

Most mornings when Cutie woke up, she was as bright-eyed as the day. But Cutie's mother and father? They were beat.

Then one night, Cutie's mother and father found the Trusty Trinket toy catalog. On page 647 was a talking doll named Night Owl.

Child can't sleep? Driving you crazy?
Night Owl is the perfect companion.
Guaranteed to put a kid out till dawn.

"Now *that's* a toy worth having," said Cutie's father.

"Let's order it *now*," said Cutie's mother.

Soon Night Owl belonged to Cutie. He had fluffy feathers. He had eyes as bright as the stars. He came with a hat and wings made of satin.

Night Owl's package instructions were simple:

PUSH NIGHT OWL'S BELLY, AND HE'LL SING YOU TO SLEEP.

"Go ahead, give it a try," Cutie's parents encouraged her.

When Cutie pushed Night Owl's belly, all the doll said was, "Sweet dreams."

"You call that a song?" Cutie was not impressed.

Cutie's new toy didn't put her to sleep, but it did keep her busy in her bedroom.

She pushed its belly again and again. But Night Owl always said the same thing. "Sweet dreams."

Soon Cutie's room grew dark. Then, all of a sudden, the bird went quiet.

Cutie pushed and pushed and pushed. Then she gave Night Owl a good shake. "You're supposed to *sing*!" Cutie cried.

Suddenly, Night Owl spoke. "Hey, Cutie, I only sing at the Dreamland Nightclub, where they party all night long. Hang with me and we'll go uptown together."

Cutie tugged at her nightie. "I'm not dressed right."
Night Owl said, "Dressed? Nobody gets dressed to go
to Dreamland. Why do you think they call it a *night*club?"

"But I never go anywhere without my purse."
Cutie huffed.
   "Grab your purse and let's rock," Night Owl said.

Cutie and Night Owl mounted her horse, and off
they rode. When they walked in the door,
Dreamland was as live as a bird on a wire.
    Satin Doll let loose on the piano.
    The Sandman slammed on his drums.
    And tonight the Slumber Brothers performed their
world-famous soft-shoe duet.
    "This is *some* place," Cutie said.

Night Owl grabbed Cutie by the hand. "Let's join the jam."
Night Owl and Cutie cut the rug to ribbons. Then they
sipped a nightcap, a double-chocolate cup of cocoa.

Soon it was Night Owl's turn to sing. He belted "Sweet Dreams" from deep in his feather belly. What a hoot.

When Night Owl was through, he called Cutie to the stage. "Your turn," he said. "Take the floor, Cutie LaRue!"

And Cutie did. She turned the party out. She sang with Night Owl like tomorrow wasn't ever gonna come.

Then Cutie soft-shoed with
the Slumber Brothers.

She learned to jam
on the Sandman's snare.

Satin Doll showed her
how to play the piano.

Night Owl said, "Look at you, Cutie. You're a late-night kid who doesn't quit. Let's hit the dance floor one more time!"

Cutie yawned as big as the full moon's face. "No thanks," she said, "I'm *too* tired."

Then Cutie curled up in the middle of the stage, tapped her foot a few times, and fell fast asleep.

The next morning, when Cutie's mother and father checked on Cutie, she was snuggled close with Night Owl. That night, and every night after, Cutie LaRue had no trouble going off to bed. When bedtime came, her parents didn't even have to tuck her in.

They just had to make sure Night Owl was waiting
for her on her pillow.